# DAVID
# LODGE

SURPRISED BY SUMMER

PENGUIN BOOKS

# PENGUIN BOOKS

Published by the Penguin Group. Penguin Books Ltd, 27 Wrights Lane, London w8 5TZ, England. Penguin Books USA Inc., 375 Hudson Street, New York, New York 10014, USA. Penguin Books Australia Ltd, Ringwood, Victoria, Australia. Penguin Books Canada Ltd, 10 Alcorn Avenue, Toronto, Ontario, Canada M4V 3B2. Penguin Books (NZ) Ltd, 182–190 Wairau Road, Auckland 10, New Zealand · Penguin Books Ltd, Registered Offices: Harmondsworth, Middlesex, England · 'Where the Climate's Sultry' first published in *Cosmopolitan* 1987. Copyright © David Lodge, 1987. 'My First Job' first published in the *London Review of Books*, 1980. Copyright © David Lodge, 1980. 'Hotel des Boobs' first published in *Cosmopolitan* 1986. Copyright © David Lodge, 1986. The stories have been lightly revised for this edition, published 1996. Copyright © David Lodge, 1996. All rights reserved · The moral right of the author has been asserted · Typeset by Rowland Phototypesetting Ltd, Bury St Edmunds, Suffolk. Printed in England by Clays Ltd, St Ives plc · Except in the United States of America, this book is sold subject to the condition that it shall not, by way of trade or otherwise, be lent, re-sold, hired out, or otherwise circulated without the publisher's prior consent in any form of binding or cover other than that in which it is published and without a similar condition including this condition being imposed on the subsequent purchaser · 10 9 8 7 6 5 4 3 2 1

*Summer surprised us . . .*

T. S. ELIOT, *The Waste Land*

# CONTENTS

## *Where the Climate's Sultry*

Long, long ago, in August 1955, before the Pill or the Permissive Society had been invented, four young people from England struggled inexpertly with their sexual appetites on the island of Ibiza, which, as a place of popular British resort, also had yet to be invented. Ibiza was still an exotic destination in those days, one the departing holiday-maker might let drop without self-deprecation – with, indeed, a certain air of adventurousness. It was certainly an adventure for Desmond, Joanna, Robin and Sally.

Des, Jo, Rob and Sal – thus were they known to each other, the less essential syllables of their names having worn away under continual use – had first met and paired off at a Freshers' Hop in their second week at a redbrick provincial university. Elective affinities drew them together in that milling throng of anxious and excitable youth. Each of them, unnerved by the sexual competitiveness of their new environment, was looking, half-consciously, for an agreeable, presentable companion of the opposite sex who would settle, once and for all, the question of who to 'go around with'. They chose well. Over the next three years, while their contemporaries changed partners with fickle frequency, or remained for ever starved and solitary on the edge of the dance, while all around them jilted boys took to drink, and forsaken girls wept into their tutors' handkerchiefs, while rash engagements were painfully dissolved, and nervous breakdowns spread like flu, the twin relationships of Desmond and Joanna, Robin and Sally, remained serene and stable: a fixed, four-starred constellation in an expanding and fissile universe.

Both girls were doing a general Arts degree, and the boys were doing Chemistry. Outside lectures, they formed an inseparable quartet. In their second year, as University regulations permitted, the girls rented a bed-sitting room, and here all four ate and studied together in the evenings. At ten o'clock they made a final cup of coffee and dimmed the lights. Then for half an hour or so, until it was time for the boys to return to their digs, they reclined on twin divans for a cuddle. Nothing more than a cuddle was possible in the circumstances, but this arrangement suited them well. Joanna and Sally were nice girls, and Desmond and Robin were considerate young men. Both couples vaguely assumed that eventually they would get married, but this possibility seemed at once too remote and too real to be anticipated. If three was a crowd, four was company in this situation. Indeed, while fondling each other on their respective divan beds, the two couples would often maintain a lively four-pointed conversation across the space between them.

All worked hard as Finals approached. They planned to reward themselves, and round off their undergraduate careers, with what Desmond described as 'a slap-up Continental holiday, somewhere off the beaten track', to be financed by a month's work in a frozen-food factory. It was a measure of what sensible, responsible young people they were that not one of the eight parents concerned raised any objection to this plan. They perhaps reckoned without the effect of a Mediterranean atmosphere upon placid English temperaments. As Joanna, who had prepared a question on Byron for her Finals, liked to quote, with almost obsessive frequency, in Ibiza:

> What men call gallantry, and gods adultery,
>     Is much more common where the climate's sultry.

There was no airport in Ibiza in those days. A student charter flight in a shuddering old Dakota took them to Barcelona, where they embarked the same evening on a boat bound for the Balearic Islands. Desmond and Robin sat up on deck, where the girls joined them at dawn to watch, with suitable exclamations, the white, steeply raked façade of the town of Ibiza rise slowly out of the turquoise Mediterranean. They breakfasted on rolls and coffee outside a quayside café, feeling the sun already burning between their shoulder-blades. Then they took a bus across the island, where they had booked into a pension at a more sheltered resort with a beach.

At first they were quite content with swimming, sunbathing and the other simple diversions of the little resort: the cafés and *bodegas* where alcohol was so absurdly cheap, the shops selling gaudy basket-work and leather goods, and the rather pretentiously named 'nightclubs' where, for the price of a bottle of sweet Spanish champagne, you could dance on a concrete floor to the jerky rhythm of a three-piece band and occasionally witness an amateurish but spirited performance of flamenco dancing. The young people conducted themselves with their habitual decorum and amiability, and the proprietress of the pension, who had regarded them somewhat suspiciously on their arrival, now beamed at them as they came in for the somewhat repetitive, but decent fare she served: soup, fish or veal, chips, salad and water melon.

The loss of innocence began, perhaps, with an awareness of their enhanced physical attractiveness. The pallor of study and factory work was burned away by the southern sun in a matter of days, and they looked at each other as into an artificially tinted ballroom mirror, with little thrills of pleasurable surprise. How handsome, how pretty, they were! How becoming was Joanna's freckled tan against her sun-bleached hair, how trim and limber Sally's brown limbs in her yellow swim-suit, how fit and virile the boys looked on the beach, or dressed for the evening in white shirts and natty lightweight slacks.

Then the rhythm of the Spanish day was itself an invitation to sensual indulgence. They got up late, breakfasted and went to the beach. At about two they returned to the pension for lunch, with which they drank a good deal of wine. They then retired to their rooms for a siesta. At six, showered and changed, they took a stroll and an aperitif. They dined at eight-thirty, and afterwards went out again, into the silky Mediterranean night, to a favourite *bodega* where, sitting round a bare wooden table, they conscientiously sampled every liqueur known to the Balearic Islands. Sometime after midnight they returned to the pension, a little unsteady on their feet, giggling and shushing each other on the stairs. They all went into the girls' room and Joanna brewed them instant coffee with a little electric gadget that you immersed in a cup of water. Then they cuddled for a while on the twin beds. But the hours they learned to identify as the most erotically exciting were those of the siesta, when they lay on their beds in their underclothes, replete with food and drink, sleepy but seldom asleep, dazed by the heat that pressed against the closed shutters, limp, unresisting vessels of idle thoughts and desires.

•

One afternoon Desmond and Robin were lying on their beds in their Y-fronts, Robin browsing listlessly in an old copy of the *New Statesman* he had brought with him, and Desmond staring, hypnotized, at the closed shutters, where sunlight was seeping through the cracks like molten metal, when there was a knock on the door. It was Sally.

'Are you decent?'

Robin answered: 'No.'

'In the nude?'

'No.'

'That's all right then.'

Sally came into the room. Neither boy moved to cover himself. Somehow it seemed too much of an effort in the heat. In any case, Sally's own knickers were clearly visible beneath the shirt, borrowed from Robin, that she was wearing by way of a negligée.

'What d'you want?' said Robin.

'Company. Jo's asleep. Move up a bit.'

Sally sat down on Robin's bed.

'Ouch, mind my sun-burn,' he said.

Desmond closed his eyes and listened for a while to the whispers, giggles, rustlings and creakings from the other bed. 'In case you haven't noticed,' he said at length, 'I'm trying to have a siesta.'

'Why don't you take my bed, then?' said Sally. 'It's quiet in there.'

'Good idea,' said Desmond, getting up and putting on his bathrobe.

After he had left, Sally snickered.

'What?' said Robin.

'Jo's got nothing on.'

'Really nothing?'

'Not a stitch.'


Desmond knocked on the door of the girls' room. There was no reply, so he put his head round the door. Joanna was asleep, with her back towards him. Her buttocks, white against her tan, shone palely, like twin moons, in the shuttered room. He hastily closed the door and stood still in the corridor, his heart thumping. Then he knocked again, more firmly.

'What? Who is it?'

'It's me – Des.'

'Just a mo. All right.'

He went in. Joanna had covered herself with a sheet. She was flushed and her hair was stuck to her forehead with perspiration. 'Is it time to get up?' she asked.

'No. Rob and Sal are larking about in our room, so I've come to have my siesta in here.'

'Oh.'

'Is that all right?'

'Make yourself at home.'

Desmond lay down on Sally's bed in the attitude of a soldier standing to attention.

'You don't look very relaxed,' said Joanna.

'Can I lie down with you?'

'All right.' He was across the room in a flash. 'As long as you stay outside the sheet,' she added.

'Why?'

'I've got nothing on.'

'Haven't you?'

'It's so hot.'

'It is, isn't it.' Desmond took off his bathrobe.

*'And so they make a group that's quite antique . . .'*

'What?'

*'Half-naked, loving, natural and Greek.'* Joanna blushed slightly. 'Byron.'

'Him again! Pretty sexy type, wasn't he?'

'Yes, he was, as a matter of fact.'

'Like me,' said Desmond complacently, stroking Joanna through the sheet.

The next day, after lunch, there was a little embarrassed hesitation on the landing before they separated for the siesta. Then Desmond said to Robin, 'Why don't you go in Sally's room this time?' and a few moments later Robin and Joanna passed each other in the corridor wearing bathrobes and

bashful smiles. The same thing happened the next day, and

the day after that. They formed a silent, thoughtful group over the late-night coffee. The communal cuddle was a rather perfunctory ritual now: all had tasted headier pleasures in the afternoon. Afterwards they found it difficult to sleep in their hot, dark bedrooms.

'Des . . .'
  'Mmm?'
  'Have you ever, you know . . . ?'
  'What?'
  'Done it with a girl.'
  After a longish pause, Desmond answered. 'I don't know.'
  Robin sat up in his bed. 'Either you have or you haven't!'
  'I tried once, but I don't think I did it properly.'
  'What, you and Jo?'
  'Good God, no!'
  'Who then?'
  'I've forgotten her name. It was years ago, I was camping, with the scouts, in the Dales. These two local girls used to hang about the camp at night. Me and this other chap went for a walk with them one night. The one I was with suddenly said, "You can do me if you like."'
  'Ye gods,' Robin breathed enviously.
  'It was sopping wet on the ground, so we stood up against  9

a tree. I kept slipping on the roots and I couldn't see a damned thing. Afterwards she said, "Well, I wouldn't give thee a badge for that, lad."'

Robin laughed aloud and gratefully.

'What about you?' Desmond inquired.

Robin was glum again. 'Never.'

'What made you ask?'

'These afternoons with Sal. It's driving me mad.'

'I know. We nearly went the whole way today.'

'So did we.'

'We'd better give it some serious thought.'

'I think about it all the time.'

'I mean precautions.'

'Oh. Yes, I suppose it would be risky.'

'Risky!'

'You didn't bring any with you, I suppose, what d'you call 'em . . .'

'French letters?'

'That's right.'

'Me?'

'Well, someone of your experience . . .'

'What experience?'

'In the scouts.'

'Don't be daft.'

'What shall we do, then?'

'We could try the local shops.'

'Hmm.' Robin was doubtful. 'Catholic country, you know. Probably illegal. Anyway, what are they called in Spanish?'

'Let's look in the phrase book.'

'Good idea.' Robin jumped out of bed and turned on the light. Together they bent their heads over *The Holiday-maker's Spanish Phrase Book.*

'What will it be under?'

'Try "The Chemist's Shop." Or "At the Barber's."'

'Oh yes,' said Robin bitterly, after a few minutes perusal. 'They find room for "*I have blisters on the soles of my feet,*" and "*Please may I have a shampoo for a dry scalp,*" but when there's something you're actually likely to *need* . . .'

'Hang on,' said Desmond. 'We didn't look at "Consulting the Doctor." There's a sort of all–purpose phrase here which says, "*I have a pain in my . . .*" You don't think we could adapt that?'

'No.' Robin turned off the light and groped his way back to bed. Some time later he found himself staring into the light and the eyes of Desmond, who was shaking him urgently, hissing the words '*New Statesman.*'

'Uh?'

'Your *New Statesman.* It has Family Planning ads in the back.'

Robin was suddenly wide awake. 'Des, you're a genius,' he said. And then: 'But there won't be time.'

'I worked it out. If we send off tomorrow, they should arrive in a week, or just over.'

'That's cutting it fine.'

'Well, have you got a better idea?'

Robin hadn't. They found an advertisement in the *New Statesman*, but it offered only a free catalogue. Not knowing the price or specifications of their requirements, they had some difficulty composing an order. But at last it was finished. In enclosing the money they agreed to err on the side of generosity. 'Let's tell them to keep the change,' said Robin. 'That should hurry things up.'

Meanwhile, however, another conversation had been going on at the other end of the corridor which rendered these labours vain. The girls broke it to them the next morning on the beach.

'Jo and I had a serious talk last night,' said Sally. 'And we agreed that it's got to stop, before it's too late.'

'What's got to stop?' said Robin.

'Why?' said Desmond, who saw no point in pretending not to understand.

'Because it isn't right,' said Joanna.

'We all know it isn't,' said Sally.

The two boys were sulky and taciturn over lunch. Afterwards they went grimly to their room for the siesta, and the

girls to theirs.

'Oh dear,' said Sally. 'I do hope this is not going to spoil the holiday.'

'What we need,' said Joanna sensibly, 'is a change of scenery. Let's go into Ibiza tomorrow.'

So the next day they took the bus into the town. There was a small crowd of people gathered on the quayside, watching a rather rakish-looking, black-painted yacht. Robin caught the name of a famous film-star.

'Ooh!' said Sally. 'Let's wait and see if he comes ashore.'

They hung around for a while, but the famous film-star did not appear. Once a well-developed young woman in a two-piece swimsuit stared haughtily at them for a few moments from a hatchway and then withdrew.

'No wonder he doesn't want to come ashore,' said Desmond.

'Let's go, I'm bored,' said Joanna.

They wandered round the old town, doing their best to avoid the gruesome cripples who begged on every street corner. They climbed up a succession of steep, smelly alleys festooned with washing, and found themselves on the parapet of a kind of fortress overlooking the harbour. Inside the fort was a little archaeological museum, with flints and shards and some coins and carvings. Joanna and Sally went to the Ladies. Sally emerged first, somewhat shaken by the

13

experience, and found the boys poring over a glass display case.

'What have you found?'

Robin smirked. 'Take a look.'

The case contained a number of tiny, crudely fashioned clay figures, with grossly exaggerated sexual organs: huge phalluses, jutting breasts and grooved, distended bellies.

'Oh,' said Sally, after staring at them blankly for a while. 'Fancy putting things like that in a museum.'

'What is it?' said Joanna, joining them.

Desmond made room for her. 'Fertility whatnots,' he said.

'We don't seem to be able to get away from the subject, do we?' Sally said to Joanna, as they left the museum. The two boys were sniggering together behind them as they walked arm in arm down the hill.

For the rest of the day, and all the next day, Desmond and Robin kept together, leaving the girls to each other's company, implying that if that was how it was to be for the siesta, that was how it had better be all the time. The girls were well aware of this message, and it made them restive and unhappy. At dinner Robin and Desmond talked animatedly about the molecular structure of clay and its possible application to the dating of fertility whatnots, and in the *bodega* afterwards they pursued the same topic over Green Chartreuse. Two young Americans in violently checked

Bermuda shorts asked politely if they might sit at the same table, for the bar was crowded, and were drawn into the discussion. Robin and Desmond described the treasures of the Ibiza museum in eloquent detail, while the two Americans grinned at the two girls.

'We can't go on like this,' said Sally that night.

'But we can't change our minds,' said Joanna. 'Can we?'

'I've been thinking,' said Sally, 'it would be different if we were engaged.'

'Yes,' said Joanna thoughtfully, 'it would, wouldn't it.'

So the next day they all got engaged. It was unofficial – they would wait till they got home to tell their parents – but it was quite properly done. Each girl chose a cheap ring, 'to be going on with' from a stall in the market, and wore it proudly on her third finger. In the evening they had a celebration dinner in a restaurant, and sentimentally held hands between courses. The two Americans, who happened to be in the same restaurant, noticed the rings and offered their congratulations.

'I'm ever so glad we decided to get engaged,' said Joanna to Desmond the following afternoon, 'aren't you, Des?'

'Oh yes.'

'Not just so we can siesta together?'

''Course not.'

'It's different, somehow, being definitely engaged. I mean, *before*, I was never quite sure whether we weren't just doing it for pleasure. But now I know it's for love.'

'Pleasure too.'

'Oh, yes, pleasure too. Oh Des!'

'Oh, Jo!'

'Goodness,' Sally murmured, averting her eyes, 'you look just like a fertility whatnot.'

'I feel like one,' said Robin.

It was not long before they all realized that they had not solved their problem, but merely raised the price of its solution. One fateful question hung over their waking hours, and their waking hours were many, for they discussed it late into the hot nights.

'Sal.'

'Yes?'

'We nearly did it today.'

'We nearly do it every day.'

'No, I mean really. I told Des, "If you want to, I couldn't stop you."'

'Gosh, what happened?'

'Well he was ever so sweet. He said, "I'll give you ten to think it over," and went and sat on the other bed.'

'And?'

'When he'd finished counting, I'd sort of come round.'

'Didn't you wish you'd counted faster?' said Robin.

'Not really,' said Desmond. 'I sobered up myself. I began to think, what if Jo got pregnant? I mean, we're no nearer to getting married than we were last week.'

'It's about time those things came from the *New Statesman* place,' said Robin. 'There's not much time left.'

'Well, there aren't many days left now, anyhow,' said Joanna. 'It will be easier when we get back to England.'

'Yes, everything seems different Abroad.'

'*What men call gallantry and gods adultery . . .*'

'It would be fornication, not adultery,' said Sally, who was getting rather tired of this quotation.

The next day, Desmond received a plain brown envelope in the mail and took it to his room, followed eagerly by Robin.

'There's nothing in it,' Desmond said grimly, 'I can feel.' He tore the envelope open and took out a letter and his cheque.

'Blast!'

'What do they say?'

'We regret that regulations prohibit us from conveying our goods to the Spanish Republic.'

'I told you,' said Robin. 'It's a Catholic country.'

'Fascist swine,' said Desmond. 'Inquisitors. Police State.' He worked himself up into a frenzy of anti-Spanish sentiment. 'Priest-mongers! Hypocrites!' He leaned out of the window and cried, 'Down with Franco! Up Sir Walter Raleigh!'

'I say, steady on,' said Robin.

The two Americans, who were passing in the street below, looked up wonderingly. Desmond waved to them. 'Rob,' he said over his shoulder, 'I wonder if those Yanks have any.'

'They've got Things,' Sally said to Joanna that night.

'I know.'

'We must stick together, Jo.'

'Yes.'

'Why not?' said Robin. 'It's perfectly safe.'

'I'm sure it is,' said Sally. 'But . . .'

'But what?'

'Well, I think we should keep one thing for when we get married.'

'But we can't get married for years.'

'All the more reason.'

'I suppose you think I wouldn't respect you,' said Desmond. 'Afterwards.'

'Oh, no, Des, it's not that.'

'I'd respect you more. For having the courage of your convictions.'

'But I don't have any convictions. Just a feeling. That we'd regret it.'

Desmond sighed and rolled away from her. 'You disappoint me, Jo,' he said.

'D'you think we're being unreasonable?' said Joanna that night.

'I think *they're* being unreasonable,' said Sally. 'After all, we've given in and given in.'

'You've got to draw the line somewhere.'

'Exactly.'

'I suppose it's different for a boy, though,' said Joanna.

'Rob', said Sally, 'says it's like holding your thumb against a running tap.'

Lying in the darkness, the two girls silently pondered this eloquent image. Joanna flapped her sheet to make a breeze. 'It seems hotter than ever,' she said.

And so, as the holiday drew towards its close, tension increased and found relief in a debauch of talk. They no longer bothered to maintain the convention that each couple conducted its intimate life in private: they brought their common problem out into the open and discussed it – on the beach, at meals, over drinks – with a freedom and sophistication that amazed themselves. 'I think we're all agreed that there's no special virtue in virginity *qua* virginity,' Robin would say, with the air of a chairman who sensed that he had the feeling of the meeting, and they would all nod sagely in agreement. 'In fact, I think one could safely say that *some* sexual experience before marriage is positively desirable.'

'Yes, I agree,' said Sally, 'in principle. I mean the first time could be an awful shambles if neither of you knew what you were supposed to be doing, and why should the girl always be the innocent one? That's old hat.'

'But don't you think', said Joanna, 'that it's a shame if there's nothing to look forward to when you get married? I mean, if it's just legalizing what's already happened?'

'The trouble is,' said Desmond, 'that we got attached to the people we want to marry before we had a chance to get sexual experience with anyone else.'

'You know, Des, that's rather neatly put,' said Sally.

It was like old times again: the relaxed camaraderie of their undergraduate days was restored. There was again a lively four-pointed discussion over coffee late at night. But it was not until the penultimate night of their holiday that they faced the fact that there was only one solution to their dilemma.

They were sitting on the beds in the girls' room, flushed and bright-eyed from the drinks they had consumed in the course of the evening (rather more than usual, for they were getting reckless with their pesetas) when Desmond put it to them.

'It seems to me', he said, swirling the coffee dregs in his tooth mug, 'that if we all want to have the experience, but we don't want to anticipate marriage, and we don't want to go with tarts or gigolos –'

'Certainly not,' said Sally.

'What a revolting idea,' said Joanna.

'Then there's only one possibility left.'

'Swap, you mean?' said Robin.

'Mmm,' said Desmond. To his surprise, nobody laughed. He glanced swiftly round the group. Their eyes did not meet his, but beneath lowered lids they gleamed with the sly wantonness of children who have been left alone together, for too long, in an empty house, on a wet afternoon.

Some two hours later, Sally knocked at the door of the room she shared with Joanna. Robin opened it almost immediately, pale-faced and staring wildly.

'Have you finished?' Sally whispered.

He nodded spastically, and stood aside to admit her. She avoided his eyes. 'Goodnight,' she said, and almost pushed him into the corridor. He was still standing there, staring at her, as she closed the door. Inside the room, Joanna was sobbing quietly into her pillow.

'Oh God,' said Sally, 'don't tell me you did it?'

Joanna sat up. 'Didn't you, then?'

'No.'

'Oh, thank *heavens*!' Joanna collapsed into renewed tears. 'Neither did we.'

'What are you crying about, then?'

'I thought you and Des ... You were such a long time.'

'We were waiting for *you*. Des was frantic.'

'Poor Des!'

'I wonder how you can stand him.'

'Rob was *beastly*.'

'Was he?' Sally sounded pleased.

'Oh Sal, what happened to us? How could we ever dream of doing anything so awful?'

'I don't know,' said Sally, getting into bed. 'Perhaps it's this place. Sultry and adultery and all that.'

'You said it wasn't adultery,' Joanna sniffed.

'It would have been jolly near it this time,' said Sally.

When Robin returned to his room, Desmond was smoking in the darkness. Robin silently took off his robe and got into bed.

'All right?' said Desmond, clearing his throat.

'Yes,' replied Robin. 'And you?'

'Oh, fine.' He added after a pause, 'I meant, you got on all right?'

'Yes. That's what I thought you meant.'

'Oh.'

'Is that what you thought *I* meant when you said, "Fine?"'

'Yes.'

'That's what I thought. What I meant.'

'Ah.' Desmond stubbed out his cigarette. ''Night then.'

'Goodnight.'

They turned and faced their respective walls, wide awake and racked with jealousy and hatred.

Next morning they rose, dressed, and shaved in a hostile silence. Each surreptitiously disposed of an unopened packet of contraceptives before going down to breakfast.

The meal was strained. Joanna and Sally, secure in the knowledge that nothing irreparable had happened the previous night, were inclined to make light of the whole affair. It never occurred to them that Robin and Desmond had not been taken into each other's confidence. To them the boys' behaviour seemed merely boorish and unsporting; but to 23 the boys the levity of Joanna and Sally seemed heartless and depraved. When, at length, Joanna indulged in her favourite quotation, Desmond leaned across the table and slapped her face, hard and resoundingly. A sudden hush fell over the dining room. A young waiter fled, rattling crockery, to the kitchen. Joanna whimpered, nursing her flushed cheek, her incredulous eyes swamped with tears.

'Des!' Sally exclaimed. 'What a foul thing to do!'

'You encouraged her,' Robin accused.

Joanna rose unsteadily to her feet. Sally scrambled to assist her. 'You make me sick,' she hissed at Robin and Desmond. 'You know what's the matter with you? You're both impotent, so you try to prove your virility by hitting.'

Impotent? *Both* impotent? Desmond and Robin looked at each other and illumination flashed between them.

'Jo!'

'Sal! Wait!'

They rose to pursue the girls, but a little Spaniard with a moustache interposed himself and inflated his chest. The proprietress bustled in with the young waiter in tow, grasping a saucepan, like a weapon, in her hand. The girls disappeared upstairs. Desmond and Robin decided to leave the premises. As they emerged into the street, the two Americans passed in a hired pony and trap. They winked and raised their eyebrows interrogatively. One grasped his bicep and flexed his forearm; the other formed a circle with his finger and thumb.

'Oh, go to hell,' said Robin.

The quarrel was soon made up, and the misunderstanding erased. That afternoon, the last of their holiday, they took their siestas as before, Desmond with Joanna and Sally with Robin. Three months later, Desmond and Joanna got married rather suddenly, Sally being the bridesmaid and Robin the best man. A few weeks later the roles were reversed.

The two couples continued to take their summer holidays together. Having three children apiece, of approximately the same ages, they found the arrangement worked well. Now these children are themselves grown up, and fly off on package holidays for the under-30s whose advertising copy is a positive incitement to sexual promiscuity. As for Des and Rob and Jo and Sal, they have all become enthusiastic golfers in middle age, and spend their summer holidays exploring the links on the east coast of Scotland, where the climate is generally described as 'bracing'.

# My First Job

You don't have to be Protestant to have the Protestant ethic, I tell my students, when we come to Weber in my survey course on Sociological Grand Theory. Look at me, I say: Jewish father, Catholic mother – and I develop an allergic rash at the mere mention of the word 'holiday', with all its connotations of reckless expenditure of time and money. Accumulate, accumulate! – that's my motto, whether it's publications, index cards, or those flimsier bits of paper that promise to pay the bearer so many pounds if he presents them to the Bank of England. Work! Strive! Excel! For the job's own sake! My students, lolling in their seats, mentally preoccupied with the problem of how to draw the dole *and* hitchhike to Greece this summer, grin tolerantly and unbelievingly at me through their beards and fringes. Sometimes, to try and make them understand, I tell them the story of my first job.

Once upon a time, in the olden days, or, to be more precise, in the summer of 1952 (so I begin), at the age of seventeen and three-quarters, I got my first job, selling newspapers and magazines off a little trolley on Waterloo Station. It was a temporary job, to fill in a few weeks between getting my A-level results (which were excellent, I need hardly say) and going to University. There was no real economic need for me to work, and the weekly wage of £3 10s od (even allowing for subsequent inflation) made it scarcely worthwhile to travel up daily from my home in Greenwich. It was a matter of principle. My father, who ran his own dressmaking business employing thirty people (which he intended to hand on to me, his only child), was dubious of the point or profit of a university education, and determined that at least I should not loaf idly about the house while I waited to commence it. It was he who spotted the advert in the *Evening Standard*, phoned up the manager of the shop, and talked him into giving me the job on a temporary basis, without even consulting me. My mother looked at the advertisement. 'It says, "suitable school-leaver",' she observed.

'Well, he's left school, hasn't he?' demanded my father.

'"School-leaver" means some no-hope fifteen-year-old from a secondary modern,' said my mother. 'It's a euphemism.' She was a well-educated woman, my mother. 'Pays like a euphemism, too,' she added. Years of marriage to my father had imparted a Jewish edge to her Irish sense of humour.

'Never mind, it will give him an idea of what the real world is like,' said my father. 'Before he buries his head in books for another three years.'

'It's true, he ought to give his eyes a rest,' my mother agreed.

This conversation took place in the kitchen. I overheard it, sitting in the dining-room, going through my stamp collection (I was totting up the value of all my stamps in the Stanley Gibbons catalogue: I seemed to be worth thousands, though I had no intention of selling). I was *meant* to overhear the conversation, and to be ready to give an answer when the substance of it was formally put to me. Diplomatic leaks of this kind oiled the wheels of family life wonderfully.

My father came into the dining-room. 'Oh, there you are,' he said, affecting surprise, 'I've found a job for you.'

'What kind of job?' I enquired coyly. I had already decided to accept it.

The next Monday morning, I presented myself, promptly at 8.30, at the bookstall, a large green island in the middle of Waterloo Station. Waves of office workers arriving on suburban trains surged across the station precinct as if pursued by demons, pausing only to snatch newspapers and magazines from the counters of the shop for the next stage of their journeys by tube or bus. Inside the shop, in a cramped and stuffy little office, seated at a desk heaped with invoices and ringed with the traces of innumerable mugs of tea, was the manager, Mr Hoskyns: a harassed, irascible little man who had evidently suffered a stroke or some kind of palsy, since the right-hand side of his face was paralysed and the corner of his mouth was held up by a little gold hook and chain suspended from his spectacles. Out of the other corner of his mouth he asked me how much change I would give from a ten-shilling note to a customer who had bought three items costing ninepence, two and sixpence, and a penny-halfpence, respectively. Suppressing an urge to remind him that I had just passed A-level Maths-with-Stats with flying colours, I patiently answered the question, with a speed that seemed to impress him. Then Mr Hoskyns took me outside to where two youths loitered beside three mobile news-stands. These were green-painted wooden barrows, their steeply-angled sides fitted with racks for displaying magazines and newspapers.

'Ray! Mitch! This 'ere's the new boy. Show 'im the ropes,' said Mr Hoskyns, and disappeared back into his lair.

Ray was a boy of about my stature, though (I guessed) about a year younger. He was smoking a cigarette which dangled rakishly from his lower lip, and which he occasionally transferred from one side to the other without using his hands, as if to demonstrate that in one respect at least he had an advantage over Mr Hoskyns. He kept his hands plunged into the pockets of an Army Surplus windbreaker, and wore heavy boots protruding from frayed trousers. Mitch (I never did discover whether this was a nickname or a contraction of a real first or second name) was very small and of indeterminate age. He had a dirty, wizened

29

little face like a monkey's, and bit his nails continuously. He wore a collarless shirt and the jacket and trousers of two different striped suits, of the kind working-class boys often wore for Sunday-best in cheap imitation of their fathers: the jacket was brown and the trousers were blue, and both garments were in a state of considerable disrepair. They looked at me in my grey flannels and the grammar school blazer which, on the advice of my mother, I had decided to 'wear out' on the job, since I would have no further use for it.

'Wotcher wanner dead-end job like this for then?' was Ray's first utterance.

'I'm only doing it for a month,' I said. 'Just while I'm waiting to go to University.'

'University? Yer mean, like Oxford and Cambridge? The Boat Race and that?' (It should be remembered that going to University was a rarer phenomenon in 1952 than it is now.)

'No, London University. The London School of Economics.'

'Whaffor?'

'To get a degree.'

'What use is that to yer?'

I pondered a short, simple answer to this question. 'You get a better job in life afterwards,' I said at length. I didn't
bother to explain that personally I wouldn't be looking for

a job, since a thriving little business was being kept warm for me. Mitch, nibbling at his fingers, stared at me intently, like a savage pigmy surprised by the appearance of a white explorer in the jungle.

Mr Hoskyns popped an angry head round the door. 'I thought I said, "Show 'im the ropes," didn't I?'

The ropes were simple enough. You loaded your trolley with newspapers and magazines, and trundled off to platforms where trains were filling up prior to their departure. There were no kiosks on the actual platforms of Waterloo Station in those days, and we were meant to serve passengers who had passed through the ticket barriers without providing themselves with reading matter. The briskest trade came from the boat trains that connected at Southampton with the transatlantic liners (remember them?) whose passengers always included a quota of Americans anxious to free their pockets of the heavy British change. Next in importance were the expresses to the holiday resorts and county towns of the south-west, especially the all-Pullman 'Bournemouth Belle', with its pink-shaded table lamps at every curtained window. The late-afternoon and early-evening commuting crowds, cramming themselves back into the same grimy carriages that had disgorged them in the morning, bought little except newspapers from us. Our brief was simply to roam the station in search of custom. When our stocks were low, we pushed our trolleys back to the shop to replenish them. Brenda, a pleasant young married woman with elaborately permed hair, who served behind the counter, would give us the items we asked for and make a note of the quantities.

I did not dislike the work. Railway stations are places of considerable sociological interest. The subtle gradations of the British class-system are displayed there with unparalleled richness and range of illustration. You see every human type, and may eavesdrop on some of the most deeply emotional moments in people's lives: separations and reunions of spouses and sweethearts, soldiers off to fight in distant wars, families off to start a new life in the Dominions, honeymoon couples off to . . . whatever honeymoon couples did. I had only very hazy ideas about that, having been too busy swotting for my A-levels to spare much time for thinking about sex, much less having any, even the solitary kind. When Ray told me on my second day that I ought to have some copies of the *Wanker's Times* on my trolley, I innocently went and asked Brenda for some. The word was new to me. As for the activity to which it referred, my father had effectively warned me off that in his Facts of Life talk when I was fourteen. (This talk was also delivered ostensibly to my mother while I eavesdropped in the dining-room. 'I never wasted my strength when I was a lad, you know what I mean?' my father loudly declared. 'I saved it for the right time and place.' 'I should think so too,' said my mother.)

Brenda turned brick red, and went off muttering to complain to Mr Hoskyns, who came bouncing out of his office, impassive on one side of his face, angry on the other.

'What's the idea, insulting Brenda like that? You'd better wash your mouth out, my lad, or out you go on your arse.' He checked himself, evidently recognizing my bewilderment was genuine. 'Did Ray put you up to it, then?' He sniggered, and shook his shoulders in suppressed mirth, making the little golden chain chink faintly. 'All right, I'll speak to 'im. But don't be so simple, another time.' Across the station's expanse, lurking beside the Speak Your Weight machine, I could see Ray and Mitch watching this scene with broad grins on their faces, nudging and jostling each other. 'And by the way,' Mr Hoskyns threw over his shoulder as he returned to his office, 'we never send out *'Ealth and Efficiency* on the trolleys.' (*Health and Efficiency*, I usually have to explain to the children at this point, was one of the very few publications on open sale, in those days, in which one might examine photographs of the naked female form, tastefully disposed among sand dunes, or clasping strategically positioned beach-balls.)

At the end of the day we took our money to be counted by Mr Hoskyns and entered in his ledger. On my first day I took £3 15s 6d, Mitch £5 7s 8d, and Ray £7 0s 5d. It wasn't really surprising that I lagged behind the other two, because they knew from experience the times and locations

33

of the trains that provided the best custom. By the following Friday, the busiest day of the week, I had almost caught up with Mitch – £8 19s 6d to his £9 1s 6d – though Ray had taken £10 15s 9d.

'What's the highest amount you've ever taken in one day?' I asked, as we left the shop, pocketing our meagre wages, and preparing to join the homegoing crowds. It irked me somewhat that these secondary modern types, even allowing for their greater experience, were able to take more cash than me. It bothered me much more than the practical joke over *Health and Efficiency*.

'Ray took eleven parn nineteen 'n' six one Friday,' said Mitch. 'That's the all-time record.'

Fatal phrase! Like the smell of liquor to an alcoholic. The job was suddenly transformed into a contest – like school, like examinations, except that one's performance was measured in £sd instead of percentage marks. I set myself to beat Ray's record the following Friday. I still remember the shocked, unbelieving expressions on Ray's and Mitch's faces as Mr Hoskyns called out my total.

'Twelve pounds eggs-*actly*! Well done, lad! That's the best ever, I do believe.'

The following day, Saturday, I noticed that Ray was assiduously working the long lines of holidaymakers queuing for the special trains to the seaside resorts, milking their custom before they ever got to the platforms where Mitch and I plied our trade. When Mr Hoskyns announced the tallies at the end of the day, Ray had taken £12 7s 8d – a new record, and particularly remarkable in being achieved on a Saturday.

Suddenly, we were locked in fierce competition. Economically, it was quite absurd, for we were paid no commission on sales – though Mr Hoskyns certainly was, and manifested understandable pleasure as our daily and weekly takings escalated. At the sound of our trolleys returning in the late afternoon, he would come out of his cubbyhole to greet us with a lopsided smile, his gold chain glinting in the pale sunlight that slanted through the grimy glass of the station roof. The old record of £11 19s 6d soon seemed a negligible sum – something any one of us could achieve effortlessly on a wet Monday or Tuesday. On the third Friday of my employment, we grossed over fifty pounds between us. Ray's face was white and strained as Mr Hoskyns called out the totals, and Mitch gnawed his fingernails like a starving cannibal reduced to self-consumption. Mitch had taken £14 10s 3d, Ray £18 4s 9d and myself £19 1s 3d.

The following week was my last on the job. Aware of this fact, Ray and Mitch competed fiercely to exceed my takings, while I responded eagerly to the challenge. We ran, literally ran, with our trolleys from platform to platform, as one train departed and another began to fill up. We picked out rich-looking Americans in the boat-train crowd and hung about in their vicinity with our most expensive magazines, *Vogue* and *Harper's Bazaar*, that cost a whole half-crown each, prominently displayed. We developed an eye for the kind of young man on the 'Bournemouth Belle' who would try to impress his girlfriend with a lavish expenditure of money on magazines that clearly neither of them would be reading. We shuffled our stocks and rearranged them several times a day to appeal to the clientele of the moment. We abbreviated our lunch-hour and took our tea-breaks on the move. In takings, Ray and I were neck and neck, day by day: sometimes he was the winner by a few shillings, sometimes myself. But the real needle match between us was on the Friday, which was to be my last day of work, since I had earned some overtime which entitled me to have the last Saturday off. Both Ray and I realized that this Friday would see the record smashed yet again, and perhaps the magic figure of £20 in a single day – the four-minute mile of our world – achieved by one or other of us.

Recklessly we raced across the station with our trolleys that day, to claim the most favourable pitches beside the first-class compartments of departing expresses; jealously we eyed each other's dwindling stocks. Like Arab street-traders we accosted astonished passengers and pestered them to buy our wares, forcing our way into intimate circles of tearfully embracing relatives, or tapping urgently on the windows of carriages whose occupants had already settled themselves for a quiet snooze. At one point I saw Ray actually running beside a moving train to complete the sale of a copy of *Homes and Gardens*.

At the end of the day, Mitch had taken £15 8s 6d, Ray £20 1s 9d and myself £21 2s 6d. Ray turned away, sick and white, and ground the cigarette he had been smoking under his heel. Mitch swore softly and drew blood from his mutilated finger ends. I felt suddenly sorry for them both. The future stretched out for me as rosy as the table lamps of the 'Bournemouth Belle'. Within a few years, I had reason to hope, it would be I who would be taking his seat for luncheon on the plump Pullman cushions; and although I didn't actually guess that before many more had passed I would be catching the boat train for the *Queen Mary* and a Fellowship in the United States, I had a hunch that such extended horizons would one day be mine. While for Ray and Mitch the future held only the prospect of pushing the trolleys from platform to platform, until perhaps they graduated to serving behind the counters of the shop – or, more likely, became porters or cleaners. I regretted, now, that I had won the competition for takings, and denied them the small satisfaction of beating me in that respect at least. But the worst was still to come.

Mr Hoskyns was paying me off: three one pound notes and a ten shilling note. 'You've done well, son,' he said. 'Sales from the trolleys have turned up a treat since you came 'ere. You've shown these two idle little sods what 'ard work really means. And mark my words,' he continued, turning to Ray and Mitch, 'I expect you two to keep up the good work after 'e's gorn. If you don't turn in this sort of sum *every* Friday, from now on, I'll want to know the reason why – you understand?'

The next day, I overheard my parents talking in the kitchen. 'He seems very moody,' said my mother 'Do you think he's fallen in love?' My father snorted derisively. 'In love? He's probably just constipated.' 'He seemed very quiet when he came home from work yesterday,' said my mother. 'You'd almost think he was sorry to leave.' 'He's probably wondering whether it's a good idea to go to University after all,' said my father. 'Well, he can come straight into the business now, if he wants to.'

I burst into the kitchen. 'I'll tell you why I'm moody!' I cried.

'You shouldn't listen to other people's private conversations,' said my mother.

'It's because I've seen how capitalism exploits the workers! How it sets one man against another, cons them into competing with each other, and takes all the profit. I'll have nothing more to do with it!'

My father sank on to a kitchen chair with a groan, and covered his face with his hands. 'I knew it, I knew it would happen one day. My only son, who I have been slaving for all these years, has had a brainstorm. What have I done to deserve that this should happen to me?'

So that was how I became a sociologist. My first job was also my last. (I don't call *this* a job – reading books and talking about them to a captive audience; I would pay to do it if they weren't paying me.) I didn't, as you see, go into business; I went into academic life, where the Protestant ethic does less harm to one's fellow men. But the faces of Ray and Mitch still haunt me, as I last saw them, with the realization slowly sinking in that they were committed to maintaining that punishing tempo of work, that extraordinary volume of sales, indefinitely, and to no personal advantage, or else be subjected to constant complaint and abuse. All because of me.

After my lecture on Weber, I usually go back to Marx and Engels.

# Hotel des Boobs

'Hotel des Pins!' said Harry. 'More like Hotel des Boobs.'

'Come away from that window,' said Brenda. 'Stop behaving like a Peeping Tom.'

'What d'you mean, a Peeping Tom?' said Harry, continuing to squint down at the pool area through the slats of their bedroom shutters. 'A Peeping Tom is someone who interferes with someone else's privacy.'

'This is a private hotel.'

'Hotel des Tits. Hotel des Bristols. Hey, that's not bad!' He turned his head to flash a grin across the room. 'Hotel Bristols, in the plural. Geddit?'

If Brenda got it, she wasn't impressed. Harry resumed his watch. 'I'm not interfering with anyone's privacy,' he said. 'If they don't want people to look at their tits, why don't they cover them up?'

'Well go and look, then. Don't peep. Go down to the pool and have a good look.' Brenda dragged a comb angrily through her hair. 'Hold an inspection.'

'You're going to have to go topless, you know, Brenda, before this holiday's over.'

Brenda snorted derisively.

'Why not? You've nothing to be ashamed of.' He turned his head again to leer encouragingly at her. 'You've still got a fine pair.'

'Thanks very much, I'm sure,' said Brenda. 'But I intend to keep them covered as per usual.'

'When in Rome,' said Harry.

'This isn't Rome, it's the Côte d'Azur.'

'Côte des Tits,' said Harry. 'Côte des Knockers.'

'If I'd known you were going to go on like this,' said Brenda, 'I'd never have come here.'

For years Harry and Brenda had taken family holidays every summer in Guernsey, where Brenda's parents lived. But now that the children were grown up enough to make their own arrangements, they had decided to have a change. Brenda had always wanted to see the South of France, and they felt they'd earned the right to treat themselves for once. They were quite comfortably off, now that Brenda, a recent graduate of the Open University, had a full-time job as a teacher. It had caused an agreeable stir in the managerial canteen at Barnard Castings when Harry dropped the name of their holiday destination in among the Benidorms and Palmas, the Costas of this and that, whose merits were being debated by his colleagues.

'The French Riviera, Harry?'

'Yes, a little hotel **near** St Raphael. Brenda got the name out of a book.'

'Going up in the world, aren't we?'

'Well it *is* pricey. But we thought, well, why not be extravagant, while we're still young enough to enjoy it.'

'Enjoy eyeing all those topless birds, you mean.'

'Is that right?' said Harry, with an innocence that was not entirely feigned. Of course he knew in theory that in certain parts of the Mediterranean women sunbathed topless on the beach, and he had seen pictures of the phenomenon in his secretary's daily newspaper, which he filched regularly for the sake of such illustrations. But the reality had been a shock. Not so much the promiscuous, anonymous breast-baring of the beach, as the more intimate and socially complex nudity around the hotel pool. What made the pool different, and more disturbing, was that the women who lay half-naked around its perimeter all day were the same as those you saw immaculately dressed for dinner in the evening, or nodded and smiled politely at in the lobby, or exchanged small talk about the weather with in the bar. And since Brenda found the tree-shaded pool, a few miles inland, infinitely preferable to the heat and glare and crowdedness of the beach (not to mention the probable pollution of the sea), it became the principal theatre of Harry's initiation into the new code of mammary manners.

Harry – he didn't mind admitting it – had always had a thing about women's breasts. Some men went for legs, or bums, but Harry had always been what the boys at Barnard's called a tit-fancier. 'You were weaned too early,' Brenda used to say, a diagnosis that Harry accepted with a complacent grin. He always glanced, a simple reflex action, at the bust of any sexually interesting female that came within his purview, and had spent many idle moments speculating about the shapes that were concealed beneath their sweaters, blouses and brassieres. It was disconcerting, to say the least, to find this harmless pastime rendered totally redundant under the Provençal sun. He had scarcely begun to assess the figures of the women at the Hotel des Pins before they satisfied his curiosity to the last pore. Indeed, in most cases he saw them half-naked before he met them, as it were, socially. The snooty Englishwoman, for instance, mother of twin boys and wife to the tubby stockbroker never seen without yesterday's *Financial Times* in his hand and a smug smile on his face. Or the female half of the German couple who worshipped the sun with religious zeal, turning and anointing themselves according to a strict timetable and with the aid of a quartz alarm clock. Or the deeply tanned brunette of a certain age whom Harry had privately christened Carmen Miranda, because she spoke an eager and rapid Spanish, or it might have been Portuguese, into the cordless telephone which the waiter Antoine brought to her at frequent intervals.

Mrs Snooty had hardly any breasts at all when she was lying down, just boyish pads of what looked like muscle, 43 tipped with funny little turned-up nipples that quivered like the noses of two small rodents when she stood up and moved about. The German lady's breasts were perfect cones, smooth and firm as if turned on a lathe, and never seemed to change their shape whatever posture she adopted; whereas Carmen Miranda's were like two brown satin bags filled with a viscous fluid that ebbed and flowed across her rib-cage in continual motion as she turned and twisted restlessly on her mattress, awaiting the next phone call from her absent lover. And this morning there were a pair of teenage girls down by the pool whom Harry hadn't seen before, reclining side by side, one in green bikini pants and the other in yellow, regarding their recently acquired breasts, hemispheres smooth and flawless as jelly moulds, with the quiet satisfaction of housewives watching scones rise.

'There are two newcomers today,' said Harry. 'Or should I say, four.'

'Are you coming down?' said Brenda, at the door. 'Or are you going to spend the morning peering through the shutters?'

'I'm coming. Where's my book?' He looked around the room for his Jack Higgins paperback.

'You're not making much progress with it, are you?' said Brenda sarcastically. 'I think you ought to move the bookmark every day, for appearance's sake.'

44

A book was certainly basic equipment for discreet boob-watching down by the pool: something to peer over, or round, something to look up from, as if distracted by a sudden noise or movement, at the opportune moment, just as the bird a few yards away slipped her costume off her shoulders, or rolled on to her back. Another essential item was a pair of sunglasses, as dark as possible, to conceal the precise direction of one's gaze. For there was, Harry realized, a protocol involved in toplessness. For a man to stare at, or even let his eyes rest for a measurable span of time upon, a bared bosom, would be bad form, because it would violate the fundamental principle upon which the whole practice was based, namely, that there was nothing noteworthy about it, that it was the most natural, neutral thing in the world. (Antoine was particularly skilled in managing to serve his female clients cold drinks, or take their orders for lunch, stooping low over their prone figures, without seeming to notice their nakedness.) Yet this principle was belied by another, which confined toplessness to the pool and its margins. As soon as they moved on to the terrace, or into the hotel itself, the women covered their upper halves. Did bare bosoms gain and lose erotic value in relation to arbitrary territorial zones? Did the breast eagerly gazed upon, fondled and nuzzled by husband or lover in the privacy of the bedroom, become an object of indifference, a mere anatomical protuberance no more interesting than an elbow or kneecap, on the concrete rim of the swimming pool? Obviously not. The idea was absurd. Harry had little doubt that, like himself, all the men present, including Antoine, derived considerable pleasure and stimulation from the toplessness of most of the women, and it was unlikely that the women themselves were unaware of this fact. Perhaps they found it exciting, Harry speculated, to expose themselves knowing that the men must not betray any sign of arousal; and their own menfolk might share, in a vicarious, proprietorial way in this excitement. Especially if one's own wife was better endowed than some of the others. To intercept the admiring and envious glance of another man at your wife's boobs, to think silently to yourself, *'Yes, all right matey, you can look, as long as it's not too obvious, but only I'm allowed to touch 'em, see?'* That might be very exciting.

Lying beside Brenda at the poolside, dizzy from the heat and the consideration of these puzzles and paradoxes, Harry was suddenly transfixed by an arrow of perverse desire: to see his wife naked, and lust after her, through the eyes of other men. He rolled over on to his stomach and put his mouth to Brenda's ear.

'If you'll take your top off,' he whispered, 'I'll buy you that dress we saw in St Raphael. The one for twelve hundred francs.'

The author had reached this point in his story, which he was writing seated at an umbrella-shaded table on the terrace overlooking the hotel pool, using a fountain pen and ruled foolscap, as was his wont, and having accumulated many cancelled and rewritten pages, as was also his wont, when without warning a powerful wind arose. It made the pine trees in the hotel grounds shiver and hiss, raised wavelets on the surface of the pool, knocked over several umbrellas, and whirled the leaves of the author's manuscript into the air. Some of these floated back on to the terrace, or the margins of the pool, or into the pool itself, but many were funnelled with astonishing speed high into the air, above the trees, by the hot breath of the wind. The author staggered to his feet and gaped unbelievingly at the leaves of foolscap rising higher and higher, like escaped kites, twisting and turning in the sun, white against the azure sky. It was like the visitation of some god or daemon, a pentecost in reverse, drawing words away instead of imparting them. The author felt raped. The female sunbathers around the pool, as if similarly conscious, covered their naked breasts as they stood and watched the whirling leaves of paper recede into the distance. Faces were turned towards the author, smiles of sympathy mixed with *Schadenfreude*. Bidden by the sharp voice of their mother, the English twins scurried round the pool's edge collecting up loose sheets, and brought them with doggy eagerness back to their owner. The German, who had been in the pool at the time of the wind, came up with two sodden pages, covered with weeping longhand, held between finger and thumb, and laid them carefully on the author's table to dry. Pierre, the waiter, presented another sheet on his tray. '*C'est le petit mistral*,' he said with a *moue* of commiseration. '*Quel dommage!*' The author thanked them mechanically, his eyes still on the airborne pages, now mere specks in the distance, sinking slowly down into the pine woods. Around the hotel the air was quite still again. Slowly the guests returned to their loungers and mattresses. The women discreetly uncovered their bosoms, renewed the application of Ambre Solaire, and resumed the pursuit of the perfect tan.

'Simon! Jasper!' said the Englishwoman. 'Why don't you go for a walk in the woods and see if you can find any more of the gentleman's papers?'

'Oh, no,' said the author urgently. 'Please don't bother. I'm sure they're miles away by now. And they're really not important.'

'No bother,' said the Englishwoman. 'They'll enjoy it.'

'Like a treasure hunt,' said her husband. 'Or rather, paperchase.' He chuckled at his own joke. The boys trotted off obediently into the woods. The author retired to his room, to await the return of his wife, who had missed all the excitement, from St Raphael.

'I've bought the most darling little dress,' she announced

as she entered the room. 'Don't ask me how much it cost.'

'Twelve hundred francs?'

'Good God, no, not as much as that. Seven hundred and fifty, actually. What's the matter, you look funny?'

'We've got to leave this hotel.'

He told her what had happened.

'I shouldn't worry,' said his wife. 'Those little brats probably won't find any more sheets.'

'Oh yes they will. They'll regard it as a challenge, like the Duke of Edinburgh Award. They'll comb the pine woods for miles around. And if they find anything, they're sure to read it.'

'They wouldn't understand.'

'Their parents would. Imagine Mrs Snooty finding her nipples compared to the nose tips of small rodents.'

The author's wife spluttered with laughter. 'You are a fool,' she said.

'It wasn't my fault,' he protested. 'The wind sprang out of nowhere.'

'An act of God?'

'Precisely.'

'Well, I don't suppose He approved of that story. I can't say I cared much for it myself. How was it going to end?'

The author's wife knew the story pretty well as far as he had got with it, because he had read it out to her in bed the previous night.

'Brenda accepts the bribe to go topless.'

'I don't think she would.'

'Well, she does. And Harry is pleased as Punch. He feels that he and Brenda have finally liberated themselves, joined the sophisticated set. He imagines himself telling the boys back at Barnard Castings about it, making them ribaldly envious. He gets such a hard-on that he has to lie on his stomach all day.'

'Tut, tut!' said his wife. 'How crude.'

'He can't wait to get to bed that night. But just as they're retiring, they separate for some reason I haven't worked out yet, and Harry goes up to their room first. She doesn't come at once, so Harry gets ready for bed, lies down, and falls asleep. He wakes up two hours later and finds Brenda is still missing. He is alarmed and puts on his dressing gown and slippers to go in search of her. Just at that moment, she comes in. *Where the hell have you been?* he says. She has a peculiar look on her face, goes to the fridge in their room and drinks a bottle of Perrier water before she tells him her story. She says that Antoine intercepted her downstairs to present her with a bouquet. It seems that each week all the male staff of the hotel take a vote on which female guest has the shapeliest breasts, and Brenda has come top of the poll. The bouquet was a mark of their admiration and respect. She is distressed because she left it behind in Antoine's room.'

50

'Antoine's room?'

'Yes, he coaxed her into seeing his room, a little chalet in the woods, and gave her a drink, and one thing led to another, and she ended up letting him make love to her.'

'How improbable.'

'Not necessarily. Taking off her bra in public might have released some dormant streak of wantonness in Brenda that Harry had never seen before. Anyway, she's rather drunk and quite shameless. She taunts him with graphic testimony to Antoine's skill as a lover, and says he is much better endowed than Harry.'

'Worse and worse,' said the author's wife.

'At which point Harry slaps her.'

'Oh, nice. Very nice.'

'Brenda half undresses and crawls into bed. A couple of hours later, she wakes up. Harry is standing by the window staring down at the empty pool, a ghostly blue by the light of the moon. Brenda gets out of bed, comes across and touches him on the arm. *Come to bed*, she says. *It wasn't true what I told you.* He turns his face slowly towards her. *Not true?* he says. *No, I made it up*, she says. *I went and sat in the car for two hours with a bottle of wine, and I made it up. Why?* he says. *I don't know why*, she says. *To teach you a lesson, I suppose. I was fed up with you. But it was a stupid idea. Come to bed.* But Harry just shakes his head and turns back to stare out of the window. *You always used to say size* 51 *didn't matter*, he says. *Well, it doesn't, not to me*, she says. *I told you, I made it all up.* Harry just shakes his head disbelievingly, gazing down at the blue, breastless margins of the pool. That's how the story was going to end: "he gazed down at the blue, breastless margins of the pool."'

As he spoke these words, the author was himself standing at the window, looking down at the hotel pool from which all the guests had departed to change for dinner. Only the solitary figure of Pierre moved among the umbrellas and tables, collecting discarded bathing towels and soiled tea-trays.

'Hmm,' said the author's wife.

'Harry's fixation on women's breasts, you see,' said the author, 'has been displaced by an anxiety about his own body from which he will never be free.'

'Yes, I see that. I'm not totally without critical acumen, you know.' The author's wife came to the window and looked down. 'Poor Pierre,' she said. 'He wouldn't dream of making a pass at any of us women. He's obviously gay.'

'Fortunately,' said the author, 'I hadn't got that far with my story when the wind scattered it all over the countryside. But you'd better get out the Michelin and find another hotel. I can't stand the thought of staying on here, on tenter-hooks all the time in case one of the guests comes back from a walk in the woods with a compromising piece of fiction in their paws. What an extraordinary thing to happen.'

'You know,' said the author's wife. 'It's really a better story.'

'Yes,' said the author. 'I think I shall write it. I'll call it "Tit for Tat".'

'No, call it "Hotel des Boobs",' said the author's wife. 'Theirs and yours.'

'What about yours?'

'Just leave them out of it, please.'

Much later that night, when they were in bed and just dropping off to sleep, the author's wife said:

'You don't really wish I would go topless, do you?'

'No, of course not,' said the author. But he didn't sound entirely convinced, or convincing.

# PENGUIN 60s

ISABEL ALLENDE · *Voices in My Ear*
NICHOLSON BAKER · *Playing Trombone*
LINDSEY BAREHAM · *The Little Book of Big Soups*
KAREN BLIXEN · *From the Ngong Hills*
DIRK BOGARDE · *Coming of Age*
ANTHONY BURGESS · *Childhood*
ANGELA CARTER · *Lizzie Borden*
CARLOS CASTANEDA · *The Sorcerer's Ring of Power*
ELIZABETH DAVID · *Peperonata and Other Italian Dishes*
RICHARD DAWKINS · *The Pocket Watchmaker*
GERALD DURRELL · *The Pageant of Fireflies*
RICHARD ELLMANN · *The Trial of Oscar Wilde*
EPICURUS · *Letter on Happiness*
MARIANNE FAITHFULL · *Year One*
KEITH FLOYD · *Hot and Spicy Floyd*
ALEXANDER FRATER · *Where the Dawn Comes Up like Thunder*
ESTHER FREUD · *Meeting Bilal*
JOHN KENNETH GALBRAITH · *The Culture of Contentment*
ROB GRANT AND DOUG NAYLOR · *Scenes from the Dwarf*
ROBERT GRAVES · *The Gods of Olympus*
JANE GRIGSON · *Puddings*
SOPHIE GRIGSON · *From Sophie's Table*
KATHARINE HEPBURN · *Little Me*
JAMES HERRIOT · *Seven Yorkshire Tales*
SUSAN HILL · *The Badness within Him*
ALAN HOLLINGHURST · *Adventures Underground*
BARRY HUMPHRIES · *Less is More Please*
HOWARD JACOBSON · *Expulsion from Paradise*
P. D. JAMES · *The Girl Who Loved Graveyards*
STEPHEN KING · *Umney's Last Case*

## PENGUIN 60s

## READ MORE IN PENGUIN

For complete information about books available from Penguin and how to order them, please write to us at the appropriate address below. Please note that for copyright reasons the selection of books varies from country to country.

IN THE UNITED KINGDOM: Please write to *Dept. EP, Penguin Books Ltd, Bath Road, Harmondsworth, Middlesex UB7 0DA.*

IN THE UNITED STATES: Please write to *Consumer Sales, Penguin USA, P.O. Box 999, Dept. 17109, Bergenfield, New Jersey 07621-0120.* VISA and MasterCard holders call 1-800-253-6476 to order Penguin titles.

IN CANADA: Please write to *Penguin Books Canada Ltd, 10 Alcorn Avenue, Suite 300, Toronto, Ontario M4V 3B2.*

IN AUSTRALIA: Please write to *Penguin Books Australia Ltd, P.O. Box 257, Ringwood, Victoria 3134.*

IN NEW ZEALAND: Please write to *Penguin Books (NZ) Ltd, Private Bag 102902, North Shore Mail Centre, Auckland 10.*

IN INDIA: Please write to *Penguin Books India Pvt Ltd, 706 Eros Apartments, 56 Nehru Place, New Delhi 110 019.*

IN THE NETHERLANDS: Please write to *Penguin Books Netherlands bv, Postbus 3507, NL-1001 AH Amsterdam.*

IN GERMANY: Please write to *Penguin Books Deutschland GmbH, Metzlerstrasse 26, 60594 Frankfurt am Main.*

IN SPAIN: Please write to *Penguin Books S. A., Bravo Murillo 19, 1° B, 28015 Madrid.*

IN ITALY: Please write to *Penguin Italia s.r.l., Via Felice Casati 20, I-20124 Milano.*

IN FRANCE: Please write to *Penguin France S. A., 17 rue Lejeune, F-31000 Toulouse.*

IN JAPAN: Please write to *Penguin Books Japan, Ishikiribashi Building, 2-5-4, Suido, Bunkyo-ku, Tokyo 112.*

IN GREECE: Please write to *Penguin Hellas Ltd, Dimocritou 3, GR-106 71 Athens.*

IN SOUTH AFRICA: Please write to *Longman Penguin Southern Africa (Pty) Ltd, Private Bag X08, Bertsham 2013.*